D0498656

THE BRIDGE OF DEATH

Darby Creek
A division of Lerner Publishing Group, Inc.
241 First Avenue North
Minneapolis, MN 55401 U.S.A.

Website address: www.lernerbooks.com

Cover and interior photographs: © Zeb Andrews/
Flickr/Getty Images (bridge); © iStockphoto.com/
appletat (silhouette).

Main body text set in Janson Text LT Std 12/17.5.
Typeface provided by Adobe Systems.

Library of Congress
Cataloging-in-Publication Data

Atwood, Megan.
    The bridge of death / by Megan Atwood.
        p.   cm. — (The paranormalists ; case #04)
    Summary: Best friends Jinx and Jackson suspect
a ghost may be responsible when several popular
students decide to harm themselves by jumping off
a local bridge.
    ISBN 978–0–7613–8335–2 (lib. bdg. : alk.
paper)
    [1. Ghosts—Fiction. 2. Supernatural—Fiction.
3. Bullying—Fiction. 4. Best friends—Fiction.
5. Friendship—Fiction.] I. Title.
PZ7.A8952Br 2012
[Fic]—dc23   2011049128

Manufactured in the United States of America
1 – PP –7/15/12

THE Paranormalists
CASE #4

THE BRIDGE OF
DEATH

MEGAN ATWOOD

THE PARANORMALISTS

Paranormalists Blog—

INVESTIGATION #03: MOHAWK AVENUE

Guest Blogger: Brian, new assistant investigator

First off, I want to thank Investigator #1 for hiring me, then giving me this post to write! I've wanted to be a paranormal investigator for a long time, so this is a dream come true. I'm sorry that Investigator #2 had to be let go, but such is the tricky business of ghost hunting.

Anyway, I get to write on the blog not only because I'm the new assistant, but also because the last case was about me. Yep—I'm #03. And I'm a doozy.

See, I thought I'd been haunted for years. Every time I was alone in the house, things would fly around and smash against the walls. My parents thought I was nuts. Actually, worse than that, they thought I was making it all up for attention and smashing things in the process. Let me tell you, my allowance has taken some hits. The Paranormalists came to my house to investigate the weird happenings.

And man, did stuff happen.

We were in mortal danger, for real. But it turns out,

NOTHING showed up on their equipment. No lights, no voices, no electromagnetic field disturbances. After that, the two investigators got in a big fight— Jinx says I have to say "because Investigator #2 was a big jerk"—and left before letting me know what happened.

I was kind of upset.

But then Investigator #2 told me what happened. Turns out, I wasn't being haunted by anyone else. I was being haunted by ME. It's called "poltergeist activity," and it happens if you're super upset and a teen.

Can you believe I have that much power? I'm kind of impressed with myself. Jinx is looking at me funny right now, but I'm just being honest. She said I have to be.

Anyway, now I get to work for the Paranormalists. I can say without hesitation that I can't WAIT for the next case. Anyone have something they need investigated? We have one investigator with awesome hair and one who has some pretty fantastic power. What more could you want from a ghost-hunting team?

The Rundown on Mohawk Avenue (a.k.a. my block):

Electronic Voice Phenomena: None

Electromagnetic Field: None

Video: Nothing on the infrared. (That's right—Jinx got an infrared camera!) Something knocked it down, so it didn't show anything being thrown around.

Temperature: Stayed pleasant

Verdict: Not haunted at all. POLTERGEIST ACTIVITY!

Jinx says that I need to say: Comment below, and as always, remember that the Paranormalists SEEK THE TRUTH AND FIND THE CAUSE! (Now that I'm on board, we'll have to think of a better tagline. Ow! Jinx just hit me.)

Signing off,
Brian, Assistant Investigator

CHAPTER 1

Haley snuggled into Jackson. Jackson caught a whiff of her shampoo and breathed in deeply. She smelled so good.

A familiar pang ran through him as he remembered what he was trying hard to forget.

He and Jinx weren't talking. Again.

But this time it was his fault.

He shifted uncomfortably on the couch, and Haley sat up. "Hey, wiggle bug. What's going on? Don't you like the movie?"

Jackson, in fact, did not like the movie. It was the kind of romantic comedy that he normally never had to watch. His mom didn't really like those movies, and his buddies would never watch something like it. Jinx would rather die than watch one. He was used to watching movies with a little more blood and a little less kissing.

"Oh, it's great," Jackson said, smiling at Haley. "I'm just getting comfortable." She seemed satisfied and lay back down on his chest. He was glad to have the shampoo smell back, but he couldn't believe it—Jinx would never have bought that explanation. She would have called him out on his "fake smile."

He wiggled around again, and Haley sat up and paused the movie. "All right, what's up?"

She raised her eyebrow at him, reminding him of Jinx. He sighed.

"The same," he said.

Haley sighed too. Jackson could see irritation skitter across her face. "I don't know how to make you feel any better—there's nothing you can do."

Jackson just wished his best friend and his girlfriend didn't hate each other so much.

He nodded. "I know. It's just . . . when you know someone for as long as I've known Jinx, if you've been best friends . . . it's like you lose an arm when they go away."

Haley crossed her arms. "Yeah. You said that. You and Janx are amazing friends."

Now Jackson was irritated. "Her name is Jinx."

Haley huffed. "Her name is *Jane*. She just tries to get attention with that name and with her stupid website."

"*Our* website. And she wouldn't need attention if you and people like you were nicer to her."

"People like me? You mean, people like you?"

Jackson closed his eyes. She was right. He was popular too. He reached out to Haley. "Let's not fight. I'm sorry I said anything."

But Haley wasn't appeased. "You know, you talk about Jinx an awful lot. Are you sure you wouldn't rather have her as your girlfriend?"

Jackson snorted. The thought of cuddling with Jinx was like the thought of cuddling with a mountain lion. "No. You're my girlfriend. And that's just how I'd want it."

Haley's face softened. She scooted closer to him. "Are you sure?"

He smiled back at her and grabbed the belt around her waist. He pulled her even closer, thoughts of Jinx fading to the background. "Promise," he said. Then he leaned in to kiss her.

Suddenly both Jackson's and Haley's phones made noise. Jackson's vibrated on the coffee table in front of them. The noise meant he'd gotten a text. He and Haley looked at each other and laughed.

Jackson said, "Nothing like a text to ruin a mood."

He leaned forward and grabbed his phone from the coffee table. Haley reached into her pocket and grabbed hers.

Jackson flipped his phone open and caught Haley smirking at him. "What?" he asked.

She laughed. "Your phone is from the nineties."

He didn't say it, but that's exactly what Jinx would say about his phone.

Haley and he read their texts at the same time. And at the same time, they both said, "Oh my god."

CHAPTER 2

Haley's face was pale as Jackson drove toward the hospital.

"I just can't believe it," she repeated for the tenth time. Jackson didn't say anything.

She went on. "I mean, Ruby! She had everything to live for!"

Jackson shook his head. Having dealt with death in his family, he truly didn't understand why anyone would try to kill him- or herself.

He pulled into the hospital parking lot.

Then he and Haley walked to the front desk for information.

"We're here to see Ruby Murphy," Haley said.

The front desk attendant looked at her computer screen and typed away. "She's on the fifth floor—the psychiatric ward. Room 504."

Jackson thought the attendant gave them an extra special look. He glared at her and put his hand on Haley's back to guide her away from the desk. They took the elevator without saying anything to each other. Jackson wove his fingers through hers, and she squeezed his hand.

When the doors opened, Haley and Jackson walked out hesitantly. Jackson had never been to a psychiatric ward. He half-expected to see cold linoleum floors, bars on the windows, and patients walking around drooling. Instead he saw a nicely carpeted room and large windows, unbarred. Two people sat at a table in the corner, playing chess. The ward was incredibly quiet.

Walking to the desk attendant on that floor, Haley and Jackson said they were there to see Ruby. The attendant—much nicer than the first—smiled at them and said, "She can meet you out here. For many patients it's nice to get out of the rooms." She called a number, spoke quietly, and then placed the phone back on the cradle.

"She'll be out in a minute. You can wait over there," the attendant said. She pointed to a cluster of comfortable-looking couches and chairs. Haley and Jackson sat down. Jackson's knee bounced, and Haley fidgeted with her hair.

After what seemed like forever, Ruby walked out. She wore sweatpants and a long T-shirt, and her face was ashen. A sling held her arm, which was in a cast, and when she brushed her black bangs back she revealed a butterfly bandage stuck over her eyebrow. Before Ruby could sit down next to them, Haley gave her a big, long hug. Then Jackson did too. Haley's eyes were streaming when they finished hugging.

Jackson put his hand on Ruby's shoulder. "How are you?" he said. He felt a little ridiculous asking—she was, after all, in a psych ward. But he didn't know what else to say.

Ruby looked at the floor for a minute and then answered, "Scared."

Jackson and Haley nodded but didn't speak. Finally, Haley said, "But you're OK now. Are you seeing someone? A psychiatrist or someone to talk to?"

She nodded, "Yes, but honestly, I don't need to."

Jackson cleared his throat. He said gently, "But Ruby..."

She wiped away a stray tear and looked at Haley and Jackson with defiance. "I know what they're saying, but I didn't try to kill myself."

"But why are they saying that, then?" Haley asked. Jackson admired how she absolutely believed her friend right away and didn't question her motives. Jinx would have never done that.

Ruby seemed to come alive with the question. "Well, I mean, I didn't mean to *try* to kill myself."

Haley's face froze in confusion, stuck in a look that Jackson was sure mirrored his own.

"What do you mean?" Haley asked.

Ruby scooted in closer. "I mean, something was on that bridge with me. And it was evil."

CHAPTER 3

"Whoa." Jackson sat back.

Haley, though, leaned even closer. "Evil?" she whispered.

Ruby nodded, her ponytail bouncing. "Definitely."

Jackson began to whisper too. "What do you mean? Did someone try to push you?"

"Not someone. Something. And it didn't try to push me, exactly . . . It's hard to explain."

"Tell us what happened from the beginning," Haley said.

Ruby looked around. "It's funny, but if I tell them what really happened, they'll think I'm crazy and I'll be stuck here for longer." She laughed bitterly, then continued.

"So, last night, Robert and I got in this huge fight and we broke up." Jackson couldn't help himself—he looked at Haley. This wasn't starting well—that sounded like a motive for jumping.

Ruby saw the look and said impatiently, "I know how it sounds, but no way would I try to hurt myself over a guy. Especially a guy from high school." She rolled her brown eyes, and Jackson got a glimpse of the old Ruby: the Ruby who was full of life and liked to date college guys.

"Anyway, I needed to get out of the house and take a walk, so I walked a way I normally don't. I was arguing with Robert in my head, and I didn't really pay attention to where I was going. All of a sudden I found myself on the St. Johns Bridge. It was so beautiful out. The river right below me, the lights twinkling. I don't know if I'd ever noticed it before."

She shivered as if to shake herself out of it. "Anyway, that's when I felt it."

"Felt what?" Haley asked.

"It." Ruby looked into Jackson's eyes. "I felt *It*. There was another presence there, I know it. And I know you believe in that stuff too. I've seen you hanging around that weird girl . . ."

Automatically, Jackson said, "Her name is Jinx."

Haley added, much too quickly and with irritation in her voice, "I believe in that stuff too."

Ruby looked at Haley with surprise. "I didn't know."

Haley flipped her hair back. "Well, I don't need the attention that some people with websites need."

Jackson's face burned, and he started to stand up. Ruby's face went ashen again, and she said, "I'm sorry, really. It's just, like, a kneejerk reaction is all. I kind of want to talk to Jinx about this stuff."

Haley said quietly, "I'm sorry, too."

Jackson sat down again, but his jaw still felt tense. Ruby went on without any more prodding. "Anyway," she said quickly, "all of a sudden, I felt sad. I mean, sadder than I've ever felt before. I wasn't mad anymore. I just felt heavy, like this huge weight had settled on me and I'd never get it off."

"That sounds like depression to me," Jackson said. His voice sounded hard to his own ears.

Ruby went on, "I know. It's hard to explain, though. The feelings didn't come from me. I mean, my first reaction to things is to be *mad*, not sad. I hardly ever get sad!"

This sounded true to Jackson—Ruby was a lot of things, but he'd never seen her depressed. She could be mean, hyper, angry . . . but not once had he seen her down.

"So you're saying someone—or some*thing*—made you feel sad. Pushed emotions onto you?"

Ruby nodded furiously. "Exactly," she said. "Look, I'm not the type to try to harm myself." She smiled, and Jackson saw the old Ruby again. "I mean, look at me!" She made a sweeping gesture along her body. Haley laughed, and so did Jackson.

He rubbed his chin. "So then what happened?"

"Well, then the thoughts started happening," Ruby said. "Like, I would never be happy again, I would never find anybody, I might as well just end it. And then the river suddenly looked so inviting. It looked so inviting I.... I just jumped."

She shuddered once again. "It's like I came to in the middle of the jump, you guys. Can you imagine? I felt so foggy when those thoughts happened, but then, as I'm flying through the air, everything became so clear. And I've never been so scared in my life!"

Tears coursed down her face, and Haley put an arm around her. Jackson shivered—he couldn't imagine. If what Ruby was saying was true—to not have control of your own thoughts and actions . . .

He sat back. "This sounds paranormal."

"It's not from this world, that's for sure," Ruby said. She sighed. "My parents are never going to trust me again. And no one will believe me. I'm so embarrassed. How am I going to face anyone at school?" Ruby paused, then looked up at Jackson. "Do you think that your friend, uh . . . Jinx, right? Do you think she would look into this? You can talk to your friend about it, right?"

Jackson let out a breath. "Well, that's easier said than done."

CH 4 TER

One of the things about being notorious but not popular, Jinx found out, was that news didn't reach you until the last possible moment. She didn't hear about what happened until the news had traveled around the school. *Twice, probably,* she thought. And she only heard it through Brian.

Jinx was standing at her locker, staring thoughtfully at the *Fringe* poster in the door, when Brian came bounding up to her. She sighed. Though she was glad to have him on the team—she thought—he could be so hyper sometimes. Every time she went to her locker, he was somehow there. She wondered if he actually went to any classes . . .

"Guess what," he said. He stood so close that Jinx had to back up.

"You have mono," she said, searching for books in her locker.

Brian snorted. "No, you have to kiss someone for that, I thought." He blushed so red Jinx thought his head might explode. He kept looking at her funny, so she bit: "What?"

"What?"

Jinx huffed. "You said, 'Guess what,' so I'm asking . . . what?"

"Oh, yeah." Brian leaned in, and Jinx tried to back up again, but her back had already hit the wall of lockers, so she endured him.

"So, get this. You know Ruby Murphy?"

"I'm already bored. Who cares about her?" She slammed her locker door, making Brian jump.

He grabbed her arm as she started to walk. "No, wait, this is awesome!"

She scowled and shook her arm out of his grip. Then she plastered the most bored look she could muster on her face. "Well?" she asked.

Brian whispered, "She tried to kill herself over the weekend."

That stopped Jinx. She was not bored anymore.

"Oh my god." She twisted her lip and looked down the hall. She was no fan of Ruby Murphy's. Of all the crappy popular people, Ruby might have taken the crap-cake for being the crappiest. Well, a close second to Haley. But she never thought in a million years the girl would try to end her life. For one thing, Ruby seemed to love herself waaaaayyy too much for that.

This called for an emergency Twizzler. Enemy or not, the news about Ruby was emotionally jarring. Jinx reached into her pack and pulled out the secret stash she kept in there just in case.

The bell rang, but Jinx didn't move. She asked Brian, "How? And how did you find out?"

Brian shrugged and blushed a little again. "Those freshmen who liked my site still tell me stuff sometimes." Jinx and Brian had first met after Brian attempted to start his own rival paranormal-investigation blog.

Brian continued, a weird glint in his eye. "I guess she tried to jump off a bridge. St. John's or St. Joseph's or something? Anyway, she splatted on the water and broke her arm. But that's it, can you believe it? How bad do you have to suck to try something like that and *fail*?" He started laughing, and Jinx stared at him in disbelief.

"Dude . . . that's just . . ." But she had no words. She couldn't believe how awful he was being. Ruby was not her friend, but she was a person.

Brian said, "I know! That's just so lame! But what do you expect? People like Ruby can't do anything right, evidently. I should tell her I can help her with the jump next time." His eyes clouded over, and Jinx shivered.

Before she could say anything, the last bell rang, signaling that she was late for class.

Without another word to Brian, Jinx pivoted on her heel and walked briskly to class, chewing with fury on her Twizzler.

Maybe inviting Brian to be a Paranormalist had been a bad idea. Maybe she didn't know him all that well after all.

For the millionth time since their fight, Jinx was furious at Jackson again. This was all his fault—the fact that she had to hire Brian in the first place had everything to do with Jackson betraying her. Of all the people her best friend could have dated, he had to date Haley, Jinx's arch-nemesis since the seventh grade. Why her? Was he trying to hurt Jinx on purpose? Though Jinx was not much of a crier, these thoughts always brought a lump to her throat. She had just thought she meant more to him, was all. She should have known better. Even someone like Jackson—kind, compassionate, loyal—still sucked deep down. It was a hard pill to swallow, but she now had the proof to back up her disdain for the rest of her high school. If Jackson sucked, what hope was there for anyone else?

Jinx slid into her seat in geometry while the teacher's back was turned, thrilled she'd dodged a bullet. Her cheeks were full of Twizzlers, and the person across from her started staring.

"Wha?" she asked.

With his back still turned, her geometry teacher said, "Ms. Wright, you're tardy. You can see me after class for a slip to take the counseling office."

Jinx swallowed. This just wasn't her day.

Jinx sat on a counseling-office chair, bouncing her knees up and down. She was missing lunch just to hand in a slip that would get her in trouble. And worse, Jackson worked in the counseling office during the lunch hour. Her only consolation was that he always had to run around delivering notes to people in classes. She hoped he had a busy day today.

Just as she thought the thought, Jackson walked in the door.

"Oh, hey Jackson," Jinx said. "Betray anyone today?"

Jackson closed his lips for a second before replying. "Jinx . . ." he said quietly.

She widened her eyes innocently. "What? It's almost noon. Just haven't had time yet?"

Jackson cleared his throat. "Jinx, I need to talk to you."

Jinx shook her head and pretended to be looking through her backpack. "Nuh-uh. No way. The time for talking is over."

"I need to talk to you about something besides our fight."

Jinx whirled to him. "Fight? No, this is more than a fight. This is the end of our friendship."

Jackson's shoulders slumped. She felt somewhat guilty, then felt glad that she'd hurt him. She was hurting, and so should he. But then Jackson sat up straight again, resolve stiffening his spine. "You would throw away sixteen years of friendship just because you don't like my girlfriend?"

Jinx couldn't help it. Tears stung her eyes. He had used the word *girlfriend*. It was more serious than she'd thought.

She fought the tears away and called on the one emotion that never let her down: anger.

Standing up, she yelled, "You *knew* I hated her. She has been nothing but *awful* to me for years, and you still are dating her. How can you like someone like her? She is not a good person!"

Jackson stood up too, a vein pulsing in his temple. "If you gave her half a chance, maybe you'd see that she is a good person. And how can you say that when you're hanging around that psycho, Brian?"

Jinx's mouth dropped open. "A good person? *A good person?* You don't remember seventh grade, when she invited the *entire class* to a party except for me? Or how she says mean things to me constantly in English class? *Or how she calls me a freak?*"

A counselor peeked through the crack of her office doorway at the two of them. But Jinx couldn't have cared less. She had never been so hurt in her life.

Jackson shot back, "You *want* to be known as a freak!"

The counselor stepped gingerly into the office, and Jinx could see she was going to say something to them. Before she could, Jinx shot back at Jackson, "God, Jackson, she's already rubbed off on you. I guess you are just like all the other popular kids—you'll do whatever they do just to fit in!"

At that moment, Ms. Martinez, the school principal, rushed in and stopped short when she saw the counselor. Ms. Martinez didn't seem to even notice Jinx and Jackson.

"Oh, Gloria, I'm glad I caught you." She sounded out of breath. The counselor waited for her to continue. Worry lines scrunched her forehead, and her normally perfect hair was frazzled. Jinx had never seen her so harried before. Ms. Martinez took a deep breath and said to the counselor, "We need you to start seeing students—I'm afraid we're looking at the beginning of an epidemic."

The counselor looked confused. Despite herself, Jinx looked to Jackson. Then she remembered that she hated him and scowled and turned away.

Ms. Martinez went on, her face grave. "Gloria, there's been another tragedy." She took a deep breath. "Another student has jumped off the St. Johns Bridge."

CHAPTER 5

In English class, a class Jinx had never liked but now dreaded because she had to sit behind Haley, Jinx listened in on the conversations around her.

News of the second jumper had spread like wildfire. Not just because it was juicy news, Jinx knew. But because it was yet another popular kid. This time a boy— Hunter McMann.

Jinx couldn't believe it. She had always thought of popular kids as lemmings, but she didn't think they'd ever act like actual, well, lemmings.

Haley's friend across the aisle, Maddie, was saying, "I can't believe Ruby and then Hunter would do this. How lame do you have to be to try to off yourself? I mean, get a grip." The girl wrinkled her nose. "I even used to like Hunter. Thank God I gave that up before he decided to be a psycho."

Jinx could have punched the girl. She was saying this stuff about her friend? What did she say about her enemies? She shook her head and continued doodling in her notebook. She couldn't wait to hear what shallow, awful thing Haley had to say in response. Anger burned through her. What was it that Jackson saw in that girl?

Haley was quiet for a minute. Then she said to her friend, "That's an awful thing to say."

Jinx's ears perked up. What now?

"What?" Maddie said.

"I think that's an awful thing to say," Haley continued. "What if they're really hurting?"

Maddie stammered, "I-I-I just was making a joke."

Haley waved her hand. "Whatever. Anyway, I think there's way more to it than a couple of suicide attempts. I think there's something bigger going on."

For some reason Jinx couldn't fathom, Haley turned around and looked at her pointedly. Out of instinct, Jinx said, "What do *you* want?"

The bell rang, and their English teacher breezed in. Jinx thought about the encounter through the entire class. Why had Haley looked at her at the end? Weirder still was how Haley had defended someone.

Something was definitely up.

Jinx got to find out what not two hours later.

Brian bounded up to her again at her locker. Jinx chewed on a Twizzler and tried to avoid looking at him.

Brian pointed to the Twizzler. "Those will rot your teeth out, you know."

As if Jinx hadn't gotten that speech a

million times. And 999,999 of those times had been from Jackson. The thought immediately put her in a bad mood.

The day had seemed incredibly long, and Jinx was ready to go home and work on the Paranormalists site. To think about something that didn't involve the confusing living people she had to deal with a on a day-to-day basis. She'd rather work with the formerly alive. She shuddered at the thought a second later—that could have been Hunter or Ruby.

Brian's eyes were twinkling. "You heard about McMann, right? Another one bites the dust! Or I should say water?" He cackled gleefully, then got serious. "I guess he survived too. Really, this jumping-off-a-bridge thing isn't very effective. Maybe we should brainstorm a list of some other strategies."

Jinx slammed her locker. "Brian, dude, that is not cool."

Brian's face scrunched in confusion. "Jumping off a bridge? I know. I mean, it takes some guts, but—"

Jinx cut him off. "I mean, it's not cool for you to say things like that. They tried to kill themselves, Brian. That's a big deal. I don't care how much you don't like someone, you shouldn't want them dead."

Brian recoiled like she'd hit him. "Jeez, someone can't take a joke."

The sentence echoed what Maddie had said in English. Jinx sighed. She was suddenly incredibly tired. "I'll call you later, OK? We'll talk about cases coming up."

Brian, still looking angry, said, "Fine. Whatever," and pivoted on his heel.

Relieved to be out of his crazy company, Jinx turned around and almost ran straight into Haley. The last person she wanted to deal with.

"We need to talk," Haley said.

Jinx raised her eyebrows. "Oh, do we? I don't think so." She turned again and prepared to walk out the double doors down the hall. But she remembered that Brian had just left that way. Haley stepped quickly in front of her.

"I know you don't like me."

"Wow, you got that, did you?" Jinx sneered. "Give the girl a prize."

"Please. Can I talk to you?"

The earnest look on Haley's face made Jinx stop. She exhaled and stared expectantly at Haley. She wouldn't admit it, but she was curious about what Haley had to say. She knew it had to be about Jackson. Jinx ran through the backlog of arguments and comebacks in her head while Haley geared up to speak.

What came out of Haley's mouth was far from what Jinx expected.

"I want to hire you and Brian."

Thoughts stopped churning in Jinx's head. After what felt like a minute, she was finally able to form words. "You. Hire. Us?"

Haley crossed her arms, and Jinx noticed for the first time that she looked pale. "Yes. I want to hire you and Brian."

"For what? Is this a joke?"

Haley uncrossed her arms and fidgeted with her hands. "Believe me, I don't like this any more than you do. But you're the only one who has the expertise and equipment. There's something going on at St. Johns Bridge, and I want you to find out what it is."

Jinx's shoulders relaxed. "Yeah, something's happening at St. Johns Bridge. People are jumping off of it. But what has that got to do with me?"

Haley's eyes got intense. "On Saturday, Jackson and I—" she stopped. Jinx's face had turned dark and stormy at the mention of Jackson's name.

Haley cleared her throat and went on. "We visited Ruby. And Ruby said she experienced these feelings . . . like, feelings that weren't coming from her. She felt a presence on the bridge."

Now it was Jinx's turn to cross her arms. "A presence, huh? That's convenient to mention, if you're embarrassed because you did something stupid. Didn't the rumor mill say she broke up with her boyfriend that night?"

"Well, yes," Haley said. "But you don't know her like I do. She would *never* do something like that. And neither would Hunter. I think something's going on."

Jinx adjusted the backpack on her shoulder. "I do know her. And I know you. I know all about people like you. You'll do whatever it takes to stay popular, and you don't care who you step on to do it. I notice that you didn't talk to me about this in English—maybe because you didn't want your stupid friend to know?"

Haley blushed and looked down at the floor.

"This is just stupid people making stupid choices," Jinx went on. "And now it's an epidemic of stupidity. You and your friends don't need a paranormal investigator, you need a psychologist." She began walking away. "Or better yet, just one original thought. If it wouldn't hurt too much." She smiled sweetly at Haley and began to walk away as Haley's phone beeped.

Two beats later, Haley called to her from down the hall. "Cynthia Jameson just jumped off the bridge, *Jane*. Maybe my friends need a psychologist, but at least we're not selfish and jaded like you. At least I *have* friends. You can't even keep your one!"

Before she could stop herself, Jinx whirled around. "Well, you won't have friends for long at this rate, huh?"

As she left the school, Jinx burned with shame, knowing she'd just turned into the very sort of person she had been so self-righteously yelling about.

CHAPTER 6

Jackson opened the front door and took Haley in his arms. She started sobbing immediately.

"What is going *on*?" she cried into his shoulder. He could feel the wetness soaking through his shirt. He rubbed her back and then let go of her so she could come inside the house.

He led her to the couch, grabbing some Kleenex on the way. His mom was a fanatic about tissues because his brother, Grant, had grown up with so many allergies. For once Jackson was grateful to have the boxes everywhere.

Haley slumped on the couch and took a Kleenex from the box. She wiped her tears away and blew her nose. It sounded like a car horn, it was so loud, but Jackson thought it was cute. If the situation wasn't so serious, he might have teased her about it.

She looked up at him, her green eyes red-rimmed and dewy. "Seriously, what is going on? Three people now? First Ruby, then Hunter, then Cynthia." She blew her nose again. "I overheard Ms. Martinez talking about a schoolwide assembly. This is getting out of control."

Jackson flopped down next to Haley and smoothed her hair. "The good thing is, no one has actually died."

Haley nodded. "That's true." She looked at him. "Do you think this could all be because of the ghost?"

Jackson sat back uneasily. "Haley . . . it's just . . . I'm not sure I one hundred percent buy the ghost theory."

She said, "What do you mean? You think Ruby is lying?" Her voice had gotten hard, and Jackson flinched. "You think Hunter and Cynthia just *also* decided to kill themselves by jumping off a bridge? Like it's some sort of new game?"

He put his hand on her shoulder. "No, I'm not saying that. It's just . . . Ruby had just broken up with her boyfriend. And you know her . . . she can be impulsive."

Haley looked glumly at the wall in front of her. Jackson went on. "I mean, maybe she did try and maybe she didn't. I think we need to talk to Hunter and Cynthia before we decide anything. And then I can check out the bridge." He got up and gave Haley a knowing smile. "I used to be a paranormal investigator, you know."

Sadness crept into Jackson as he thought back to the talk with Jinx in the counseling office, and he tried to swallow it down. Then he noticed Haley's expression.

"What?" he asked.

She looked a little bashful, and then said, "Don't be mad at me?"

"Umm, OK. What? What shouldn't I be mad about?"

Haley pursed her lips. "Well . . . I sort of tried to hire Jinx and Brian to check out the bridge."

Jackson sat up so fast he knocked over a statue on the table behind the couch. "You what?"

"It's just . . . I know Jinx is the one with the equipment, and so I thought she might be willing to take the case." She put her hands on his chest. "I know you're good at this investigating thing too, but don't we need, like, evidence and stuff?"

Jackson walked away. He wasn't mad that she hadn't asked him first. Not exactly. He just felt weird that his girlfriend and his best friend had an interaction that didn't involve him. As soon as he had the thought, he felt selfish and stupid.

"You talked to Jinx, and you don't have a black eye or anything?" he asked.

Haley laughed. "I think she probably wanted to hit me." She picked at her skirt. "And anyway, she said no. She doesn't believe that there could be anything paranormal going on."

Jackson could have saved Haley the trouble and told her that himself—whether or not he and Jinx were on speaking terms, he knew how she thought.

Haley went on, "I can't believe how selfish she can be. Really. Three people have jumped off a bridge, and she won't lift a finger."

"*I'm* not sure it's a ghost either, remember?" he said, taking a step back. But Haley barely noticed. She seemed lost in thought.

"At first I was going to ask Brian and Jinx when they were both together," she continued, "but I overheard part of their conversation."

She looked up at Jackson. "Brian seems a little weird. Like . . ." She started to search for the word.

Jackson finished for her: "Like, serial-killer weird?"

"Yes! Exactly! Jinx even kind of yelled at him because he was all gleeful about people jumping off a bridge. Can you imagine? What kind of person would be happy about that?"

Jackson felt a surge of pride in his best friend. He knew she couldn't stand all the people who had jumped off the bridge, but he bet it bothered her more that people were getting hurt. Jinx was soft on the inside. She'd always taken in strays, even as a little girl. Jackson remembered how she'd tried to help a dog with rabies one time. She was almost killed because she couldn't see the signs.

An image of Brian flashed in his head. "We have to get her away from Brian."

Haley nodded. "I think you're right. I think there's seriously something wrong with him."

Jackson took out his phone and texted Jinx.

> *Hey. I know ur mad but hear me out.*
> *At least stop hanging out with Brian. Hes*
> *a creep. I think you might get hurt.*

Haley rubbed his arm and said, "Remember, she may not write you back. She's still mad at you. If it were me, I might ignore you too." Jackson appreciated her thoughtfulness. Jinx wasn't Haley's favorite person either.

Jackson's phone vibrated—a return text from Jinx. He looked at Haley and smiled.

But then he read it.

YOU'RE the one who hurt me, remember? Brian is fine, he couldnt come close to hurting me like you did. You are not my friend. Stop txting me

Jackson sat back, stunned. Never before had Jinx been so cruel. For the first time since their fight, he thought about life without Jinx.

He was afraid he had truly lost his best friend forever.

CHAPTER 7

Haley patted Jackson's back while he took a few deep breaths. When he got ahold of himself, he sat back up. Haley looked like she was trying to be sympathetic, but Jackson could tell she was irritated.

In a soft voice she said, "Hey, do you want to watch a movie? I can make popcorn . . ."

Jackson closed his eyes as the words passed through him. He needed to think.

"Haley . . ." he began.

She sighed. "I get it. I really do. Go take

a walk and see if you can't figure out a way to get your friend back."

Jackson was surprised. "You get it?"

"Look, I like you. I think you're a great guy, and I think we could have a great relationship. And your best friend is part of your life—or at least should be—so I can see what the big deal is. I mean, if you like her, she's got to have redeeming qualities somewhere, right?"

Jackson smiled big. He touched her cheek. "I like you, too," he said. Then he kissed her.

"OK, I'm going to leave you to your thoughts," Haley said. "I'll call tomorrow, and maybe we can figure out what's going on then. Yes?"

Jackson nodded, relieved that his girlfriend understood. He knew there was more to her than what Jinx saw. More than a pretty, popular cheerleader who could come off as shallow. Now the problem was getting Jinx to see. Getting Jinx to even talk to him would be the first step.

Haley gave him one last small kiss on the lips and left. Jackson was left alone with his thoughts.

With Haley gone, the force of his sadness about Jinx hit him full-on. He paced the living room, trying to figure out what to do. Feeling like a caged animal, he grabbed his coat and put on his shoes.

Jackson needed fresh air. He needed a walk. As he headed out the door, he knew exactly where he'd walk to—the St. Johns Bridge. He might as well check it out and be useful while he stewed. Maybe inspiration would strike him as he searched for a possible ghost. He laughed at himself—a haunted bridge. Did that ever happen? Jinx would know.

The night was perfect for fall. Leaves crunched under his shoes, and the stars twinkled overhead. Portland could be cloudy in the fall, but the night was perfectly clear. And warm.

Jackson thought about how lucky it was that the jumpers had chosen that last week to jump. At least the water wasn't freezing. In winter, if the fall didn't kill them, the cold water would.

Sooner than he expected, he reached the St. Johns Bridge. He'd never noticed before how pretty the architecture was. Very few cars were passing over the bridge that night, and no pedestrians walked by. Jackson walked to the middle of the bridge, leaned against the railing, and looked down at the Willamette River. Inky and black, the water undulated slowly underneath. Jackson began to feel a little sleepy looking at it.

From the corner of his eye, he thought he saw something shimmer, but when he turned to look, nothing was there. He laughed. He was seeing ghosts where there were none. No, the bridge wasn't haunted. The jumpers were. Troubled, anyway. He sat down on the ground and thought about what it would take to make people try to jump.

As he sat, his mind started to become duller, like a slow fog was moving in. He blinked and shook his head, but the groggy feeling came on stronger. His vision became narrower, like someone had rubbed the corners of his eyes with Vaseline.

The sadness he'd felt before pressed down on him, heavier than ever. It hurt to breathe. No more Jinx in his life. No more of the person who understood him better than anyone. Only Jackson's dad had known him more deeply—and he was also gone. What would it be like to find his dad again?

Jackson stood up and looked over the railing to the rushing water. Maybe ... he could see him again. He'd be with him. What did he have to live for, anyway? All of it was pointless. School, friends, sports. Everything ...

Jackson felt the hairs on the back of his neck stand up. A crackling sort of energy began to surround him. But he didn't care. What he needed to do was jump. He looked at the black waves again. Inviting. Beckoning. That was where he should be.

Something dripped onto the railing. He was surprised to see it was a tear. He was crying, but he couldn't feel any of it. Everything seemed far away, not worth noticing. The energy shifted around him. It was like the very air itself wanted him gone. Disappeared. Drowned in the water.

He had to do it.

But first, he had to let Jinx know he was sorry.

Barely able to see, he took out his phone. Squinting, he typed out a text.

J, Im sorry. I dont deserve your friendship. Im going to jump. Its better for everyone.

He tried to reread it to make sure it was what he wanted to say, but his vision was still blurred. He pressed send. It didn't matter anyway. He needed to jump. He needed to jump now.

Putting one foot on top of the railing, he stepped up and flipped his left leg over the edge. A small steel ledge stuck out, and he stepped onto it. He brought his other leg over.

There was nothing between him and the water. Just one quick step and he'd be where he belonged.

One by one, he let his fingers peel away from the railing.

CHAPTER 8

"You've been acting creepy, that's all."

Jinx was practically running out of the coffee shop. She'd agreed to meet Brian there and talk about what happened at school. She didn't know why she'd agreed, but she had. Now she regretted it.

Slipping on her coat as she walked out the door, she turned to the right instead of toward her house. While she was out, she might as well go to the bridge. She was sure Haley and her lemming friends were full of it, but the idea of a haunting—no matter how unlikely—still appealed to her.

Brian followed her like a puppy dog. In fact, he followed so closely that he stepped on the heel of one of her Chucks. She stopped, exasperated, and he ran right into her.

She looked at him pointedly. "I need some time alone."

"Well, that's too bad!" Brian said. "I don't need time alone! I need to talk to you and figure out why you're being such a . . ."

Jinx crossed her arms, daring him to say it. She knew she had her meanest look on—the one even her mom was afraid of. It worked on Brian, too. "Being such a what, Brian?" she snarled.

"All I'm saying is you're overreacting. I was joking at school, that's all."

Jinx huffed out air. "I know that's what you're saying. You've been saying it for an hour. And what I'm saying is, I don't buy it. You looked genuinely happy to hear about people jumping off a bridge. That's seriously messed-up, Brian. And that blog post you did, talking about your powers . . . I just need to do some thinking."

Brian sneered. "I had no idea you were such a prude. You seem like you're edgy, but really, deep down, you're just a plain Jane."

Jinx's whole body went rigid. Knowingly or not, Brian had touched a huge nerve. She got right up in his face and said, "Listen, you immature little toad. I've seen what happens when people die. My best friend's dad died, and there's nothing, I repeat, *nothing*, funny or cute or good about it. You have the maturity of a deranged llama, Brian, and I'm starting to think you have a serious personality disorder too. Now *back off* and give me some air, or so help me I will scream bloody murder so loud that you'll be locked up for years!"

Brian stepped back at the force of Jinx's words. Fire burned through her, and her chest heaved. He put his hands up, pale and shaking. "OK, OK. I'll give you some space."

Jinx continued to stare at him. He turned around and walked in the opposite direction.

Good riddance, Jinx thought. That boy was bad news. She had to think of a way to fire him.

She began heading toward the bridge, which was only about six blocks away. As she walked, her iPhone twinkled—the sound she had chosen for text messages. It was from Jackson.

Hey. I know yr mad but hear me out. At least stop hanging out with Brian. Hes a creep. I think you might get hurt.

Jinx let out a grunt of frustration. How did he always know exactly when things were falling apart for her? When she wasn't mad at him, she adored that trait. Jackson could always sense, from wherever he was, whatever trouble she was in. He was almost psychic— and almost always right. At that moment Jinx could have punched him for it.

She stopped and thought about what to write. She certainly wasn't going to let him know that he was right about Brian—he didn't need to know that. In fact, he needed a little punishment. Her heart still hurt from him dating Haley, and she wanted to hurt him back. She wouldn't lie exactly, but she could stretch the truth, right? She typed in:

YOU'RE the one who hurt me, remember? Brian is fine, he couldnt come close to hurting me like you did. You are not my friend. Stop txting me

There. That would do it.

Guilt stung her, but she told herself Jackson deserved it. He was probably with Haley right now, and Haley was probably talking trash about her. Because that's what she did. She and all her popular friends.

Jinx walked slowly toward the bridge and remembered Haley's exchange with Maddie earlier. She *had* defended the idiots who had jumped . . . Despite herself, Jinx admired Haley for speaking up. Haley had taken something like that seriously, and more importantly, she had said something.

Then again, Haley hadn't talked to Jinx in front of her friend. So maybe her defense of the bridge-jumpers was just a fluke. Clearly, that's what it was. Haley was a puppet like all the other popular kids.

And she was dating Jinx's best friend.

Jinx shook the thought away. She was coming up on the bridge, and she could see a figure smack-dab in the middle of the bridge, standing along the railing. The figure looked familiar, but a fog settled right around it, clouding Jinx's view.

Jinx decided to go check out the fog. There was something very unnatural about it. Why did it only hover around that one spot? As Jinx got closer, she squinted to see if she could make out who the person was. With a start, she realized it was Jackson. Was he OK? And what was he doing on this bridge? She walked a little faster and saw that he was looking down and typing on his outdated phone, shoulders slumped.

Jinx was jogging now. Something wasn't right. Her phone twinkled again—she had a text—and she pulled it out of her pocket. The message was from Jackson.

J, Im sorry. I dont deserve your friendship. Im going to jump. Its better for everyone.

Jinx had to reread the message before it dawned on her. She looked up and saw Jackson put his foot on the railing and swing his leg over.

Without thinking, Jinx took off at a sprint, running faster than she ever had. She didn't have enough breath to say Jackson's name—she needed everything to run.

Twenty feet away, Jackson flipped his other foot over the railing.

Ten feet away, she saw Jackson look down at the water and close his eyes. Jinx's lungs burned.

Five feet away, Jinx watched as he peeled his fingers from the railing. He leaned forward toward the dark water.

Jinx caught the back of Jackson's coat just before his feet left the ledge. She pulled back with all her might, so hard she could hear Jackson choking.

Sobbing and panting, Jinx put her arms under Jackson's armpits and pulled with all her might. Jackson easily had seventy pounds on her—Jinx was a small girl, and he was a football player. But adrenaline made her strong, and she pulled him over the railing and dropped him on the cement.

Then she doubled over.

Everything hurt. Her lungs were on fire—she was pretty sure she would never be able to breathe again. Her legs felt loose, like they could fall off at any moment. Worse, she couldn't stop crying. For a girl who barely ever cried, the feeling was more than a little uncomfortable.

Splayed across the ground, Jackson shook his head like he was coming to. He put his arms through two of the poles that ran along the railing and pulled the rest of his body up, and then held his head like he had a huge headache.

Jinx had caught her breath but was still sobbing. She walked over to Jackson and began hitting him in the chest.

"What . . . were . . . you . . . thinking?! Your mom, your brothers—me! You stupid . . . what is wrong with you?"

Jackson grabbed her arms and pulled her into a hug. She sank down into him, and he stroked her hair.

"I'm OK. It's OK. I'm here."

She felt like she would never stop crying. When she finally did, she looked up at him accusatorily.

"Jackson," she said, her voice low and dangerous.

He said, "I have no idea, J. I mean it. It's like something took me over. I would never . . . !" Tears spilled out of his eyes. "My mom has gone through enough with my dad dying. You *know* I'd never make her go through something like this."

Sniffing, Jinx nodded. She was suddenly very, very tired. She laughed a little. "It sounds like," she said, sniffing loudly again, "the Paranormalists may have a case."

Jackson looked at her and smiled. Then the two of them were laughing so hard they were crying again. Jackson hugged her, and she breathed in his boy scent that was so familiar to her. He said on top of her hair, "Holy crap, girl, have you been working out? How did you pull me away?"

Jinx sat back and said seriously, "I would never let anything happen to you."

Jackson's face crumpled. "Me neither, Jinx. Me neither. I'm so sorry. I'm so, so sorry. I can't live without you, do you understand? You're my best friend. I'll do what it takes to make you happy."

"Yeah, life pretty much sucks without you, too." She smiled up at him, then hit him hard one more time. "So never, ever, ever, ever, ever do something like this again!"

"There's something here, Jinx. I swear."

Jinx nodded. "I know. When I was coming up the bridge, I saw this cloud around you. Kind of like . . ."

Jinx pointed to a spot farther along the bridge. The cloud hung around a girl sitting on the railing.

"Oh god," Jinx said. She put her hand to her mouth.

"Jinx," Jackson said, "that's Maddie Jacobson."

Maddie—the girl Haley had talked to in Jinx's English class. The one who had made fun of the people who jumped off the bridge. Jinx stepped forward to yell a warning to her.

Maddie looked at Jackson and Jinx. Even from where they sat, Jinx could see the unbelievable sadness in her face.

Before Jinx could say a word, Maddie flipped herself over the railing and fell to the water below.

CHAPTER 9

"Jinx, call 9-1-1!" Jackson was halfway down to the other viewpoint while he yelled. But Jinx had already dialed.

The operator answered, and Jinx said, "Help! A girl just jumped off St. Johns Bridge. She's in the water. Come quickly!"

Jackson began taking his coat off, and Jinx knew instantly that he was going to try to go in after her.

"Jackson!" Jinx yelled, taking off after him, still holding the phone to her ear. To the operator she said, "Hurry!"

The operator answered, "There's a unit on the scene now." And sure enough, Jinx began to hear loud splashing down below—something big coming through the water. Lights lit up the bridge, and a shrill siren signaled a boat coming to the rescue. Jackson and Jinx had front-row seats.

Jinx turned off the phone just as she reached Jackson. Beneath the bridge, Maddie was being pulled from the water on a rescue board. Jinx could hear her coughing from where she stood, so she knew the girl was all right. She sagged against the railing, and Jackson put his head in his hand.

"I didn't even see her. If I'd seen her, maybe I could have grabbed her." His face was pale and his voice wobbled.

"There's no way, Jackson. And she's going to be OK. Let's get to the hospital."

Jackson nodded, and the two of them walked up to the police officer on the bridge. "Are you headed toward the hospital?" Jinx asked the officer. "We're friends of that girl."

The officer's eyes were kind. She said, "Sure, I'll give you a ride," and opened the back door for them.

Jinx couldn't help feeling a little thrill—she'd never been in the back of a police car before. The radio emitted bursts of static, but Jinx could barely make out what was being said. The officer got in and started driving.

"How did someone get here so fast?" Jinx asked.

The officer said, "Since we've had so many jumpers lately, we've been patrolling. I'm actually surprised an officer wasn't on the bridge when it happened." She sighed. "I just don't get it. You kids have everything going for you. What would make you want to jump? At least you two don't seem to have it in you."

Jackson looked at Jinx. "Yeah. But I did have it all over me."

Jinx jumped as her phone made the twinkling text sound. For the millionth time. She looked down and saw it was from Brian. The boy just wouldn't stop.

She and Jackson had been at the hospital for over an hour. They had stayed in the background as Maddie's parents had come and visited her. Jinx had seen enough tears in the past few hours to make her never want to see them again.

Finally, a nurse came over and said, "I'm sorry, but visiting hours are over."

"There's no way we can go see her?" Jackson asked.

The nurse shook her head firmly. "I'm sorry, no. Her parents had to leave. We won't be allowing friends to go in either." The nurse shooed them to the door. As they got there, Jinx bent down suddenly and pretended to tie her shoe. She stuck a pen by the doorframe and then stood up.

"OK," she said brightly. "Thanks for your time."

The nurse looked at her suspiciously and ushered them out the door. Halfway down the hall Jinx flipped on her heel and started walking back.

"What are you doing, J?" Jackson sounded

irritated as he followed her toward the door. "We can't get back in there."

Jinx reached the door and couldn't believe it. Her pen was stuck between the door and the doorframe. It had worked. The nurse must have been in a hurry and hadn't made sure the door closed. Luck was finally on their side.

Jinx put her finger to her lips and pushed the door open slowly. They snuck in.

No one sat at the nurse's desk—another stroke of luck—so Jackson and Jinx checked the board quickly and found Maddie's room number. They made it into the room just as they saw a pair of feet start rounding the corner.

Maddie sat up in bed, pale, her hair still wet. She'd broken a leg and two ribs, and she was wrapped in bandages all over.

Jackson said, "Hey."

Maddie looked surprised for a moment, then said "Hey" back, as if she'd been expecting them all along. Tears streamed down her face.

She looked at Jinx and stared at her for longer than Jinx was comfortable with. After a while, Maddie said, "I've never been nice to you, and I'm sorry."

Jinx looked away and shrugged. She wasn't expecting that. "I'm used to it."

Maddie wiped her eyes and nodded. "I imagine you are. After tonight, though, it's important for me to be nicer. Now I know what it feels like to be depressed."

Jinx wasn't depressed, and she was about to argue with Maddie when she saw Jackson shake his head almost imperceptibly. She swallowed her frustration.

"What happened tonight, Maddie?" Jackson asked.

Maddie sighed. "I went for a walk to clear my head. I know you heard me talking to Haley in class today"—Maddie looked at Jinx again—"and I was being totally awful. But these jumpings were really getting to me."

She sniffed and went on. "So I decided to come check out the bridge for myself. And then, out of nowhere, I just got so sad. All these thoughts about how I'm worthless and it was just better to disappear. Like the water was where I belonged . . . And my head was all foggy. It's like everything cleared up only when I was falling." Maddie shivered.

Jinx and Jackson looked at each other. The similar stories and the fog could only mean one thing: something paranormal *was* going on.

Jackson said, "Listen, Maddie. I felt the same way on the bridge. And so did Ruby. And I haven't talked to them, but I bet Cynthia and Hunter felt the same way, too. I think there's something sinister on that bridge."

"Really? I mean, it really was the strangest thing. I wouldn't have believed it if I didn't feel it for myself. What do you think it is?"

Jinx twisted her lip. "We're not sure yet. But I promise, we'll get to the bottom of it." She got up and put on her coat. "Jackson, let's grab the equipment and make a plan."

Maddie caught Jinx's arm as she was about to leave. "Listen, Jinx. People are mean to you because they're jealous. You seem so strong, like you don't care what others think—and that scares people. Just remember that."

Is Maddie making fun of me? Jinx wondered. Though she'd never admit it to anyone but Jackson, her entire name change and ghost-hunting project was because of what people had thought. The earnest look on Maddie's face convinced Jinx she wasn't making fun of her, though.

Jackson said, "Get better, Maddie. We'll let you know what happens."

All the way out of the hospital, Jinx mulled over what Maddie had said. If she wasn't careful, she might start liking these people.

Chapter 10

"EVP?"

"Check."

"EMF?"

"Check."

"Night goggles?"

"Why do we need those?" Jackson said. "The bridge is lit up."

"Good point. Infrared camera?"

"Check. Though again, we don't really need the infrared part, right?"

Jinx smiled a huge smile. "No, but it's way

cool we have it, right?"

Jackson fiddled with the zipper on the duffel bag. "Shouldn't you be inviting Brian?"

Jinx sighed and flopped on the couch. She stared at the episode of *Ghost Hunters* on the TV. She always played the episodes with the sound off while she prepared for an investigation.

"I don't know. We got in a fight tonight. I think you're right—he's creepy. And he won't stop texting me."

Jackson flopped down next to her and bit his lip. It wouldn't help for him to say "I told you so." More importantly, Jackson was worried. Who knew what this Brian kid was capable of? He didn't like the idea of the kid texting Jinx over and over.

As if on cue, Jinx's phone twinkled. She shook her head. "Brian again. I'll give him this much: he's persistent."

Jackson felt his jaw tense up. *I might have to have a talk with Brian myself*, he thought.

"What do you see in her?"

Jackson's head snapped to Jinx. "What?"

"What do you see in her? Haley. What's so great about her?"

Jackson had known this conversation was coming. He just hadn't expected it right then. "There's more to her than you think."

Jinx put her elbows on her knees. "Tell me."

"Well, one time, before we got together . . . we ran into each other at the metaphysical shop on Main. I was . . ." Jackson knew this part might hurt Jinx, but he needed to tell her, "I was looking for the Ouija board."

"Yeah, why did you buy that?" Jinx stared at him intently.

Jackson took a deep breath. "I wanted to contact my dad."

He braced for the fight—he was positive that she would yell at him, that she would tell him how stupid he was in order to cover up her left-out feeling.

Instead Jinx said, almost so softly he couldn't hear her, "Yeah. I get that. I miss him too. I can't imagine what you must feel."

For the second time that night, Jackson felt tears behind his eyes. He shouldn't have been surprised Jinx understood—he knew that underneath her hard outside was a soft inside. He blinked and went on. "Haley was there looking for a Ouija board too. She wanted to contact her grandma. So we tried together."

Jinx twisted her lip back and forth. Finally, she said, "Did it work?"

Jackson shook his head. "No. But that's when Haley and I started dating."

Jinx stood up, pulled her T-shirt down, and paced around the couch. "You hurt me, Jackson. Not just because you started dating her—because you kept it from me. I don't like her, and I may never. But I'll try. I'll try because you're my best friend." She stopped in front of Jackson and said, "But listen, don't hide things from me again, got it? We have to trust each other, no matter what."

Jackson stood up and put his hands on her shoulders. "I promise. And Jinx? I'm sorry."

Jackson knew that he wasn't the only one who should be apologizing. He was allowed to have his own life and to make his own choices. But he also knew that Jinx had done as much as she was capable of. And she was right in one respect, even if she was still being self-absorbed. He shouldn't have kept the secret from her, even if it meant she would be mad.

Jinx nodded and then turned away. "Done." She was all businesslike again. And she and Jackson were back. "Now I just need to figure out a way to fire Brian."

The doorbell rang, and Jackson checked his watch. 9:30. Who would be coming over now?

Voices murmured up above. Jinx's parents had let someone in. Footsteps sounded on the stairs, and a figure rounded the corner, saw Jackson, and stopped cold.

Brian.

Jackson's whole body tightened up.

"Dude, what are you doing here?" Jinx said.

Brian looked enraged. "What am I doing here? What is *he* doing here?" He pointed at Jackson with a shaky finger.

"Brian, I don't think it's going to work out for you to be an investigator," Jinx said. "Jackson is back on. I'm sorry."

Brian's face turned red, and a vein pulsed in his forehead. He took a step toward Jinx, and Jackson stepped in front of her. Jinx huffed with impatience. He didn't care—no way was this guy getting closer to her.

"I think you need to leave, buddy," Jackson said, a threat looming in his voice.

"I'm not your buddy," Brian spat. He stared over Jackson's shoulder at Jinx, but Jackson could see he was shaking.

Brian pointed at Jinx. "You've made a huge mistake, Jinx. A huge mistake. And you'll be sorry." Brian turned on his heel and walked to the stairs. Before he went up, he said to Jackson in a mocking voice, "I'm so sorry about your friends, really. You should probably go join them—it's what all the cool kids are doing." Then he headed out of sight.

After the door slammed upstairs, Jackson heard Jinx sigh behind him. "Well, that went well."

But Jackson wasn't ready to joke. He was afraid for Jinx, afraid of what this kid was capable of.

Then the doorbell rang again.

Jinx and Jackson looked at each other, and Jinx said, "What's going on?"

Jackson said, his voice stormy, "I think I'm going to have to have a talk with Brian." He climbed the stairs two at a time, his whole body on high alert. He beat Jinx's family to the door and swung it open, his fist balled at his side. This normally wasn't Jackson's style, but nobody threatened his friend. Nobody.

As the door swung open, Jackson said, "You stay away from her, you creep. Or I'll make you stay away from her."

Then he stepped back in surprise.

On the doorstep stood Haley, eyes wide with alarm.

CHAPTER 11

"Haley." Jackson's voice was high with surprise.

"Do you always threaten guests when they come here?" she replied.

Jackson shook his head and opened the door wider. "Come in. What are you doing here?"

Haley walked in and looked around. "Maddie's in the hospital. I thought you might be here, and even if you weren't, I wanted to talk Jinx into investigating. This has to stop."

As if she knew her name had been called, Jinx bounded up the steps. "Jeez, Jackson, he's not a complete psycho, but you're acting—" She stopped as she saw Haley in her doorway. "Oh," she said, her face hardening. "It's you."

Jackson felt like his stomach was turning inside out. Two of his favorite people were caught in a stare-down. And this was them being nice.

"Uh, Jinx, Haley heard about Maddie. And she wanted us to investigate."

Jinx turned around and started back downstairs, waving with her hand for Jackson and Haley to follow. "Yeah. We're on it. She didn't have to come all this way."

As they reached the basement Haley said, "Yeah, well *she* wanted to come here. Maddie's my friend."

Jinx snorted. "Your friend you smacked down today in English. You know, the class where you wouldn't acknowledge my existence." She crossed her arms.

Jackson interjected quickly, "Haley, we were just getting the equipment together. We're going back to the bridge tonight. Something happened to me there tonight, too."

Haley's eyes got wide. "Did you get depressed?"

Jackson was embarrassed to tell the whole story, so he nodded. Haley threw her arms around him. Through her strawberry-blonde hair Jackson could see Jinx make throwing-up motions. He disentangled from Haley.

"There's definitely something going on there, so we're going to check it out."

"OK, I can drive," Haley said.

Jinx, who was in the middle of packing up her camera, said, "Whoa. No way. You're not going."

"Oh yes I am."

Jinx stepped closer to Haley, until they were nose to nose. "The last I looked, you were a stuck-up, shallow cheerleader—not a paranormal investigator."

Jackson said, "Uh, guys . . ." but both Haley and Jinx gave him such looks of fury that he closed his mouth.

"It's true," Haley said. "I'm not a freaky chick who needs to dye her hair for attention.

But in case you didn't notice, those are my friends jumping out there."

"Yeah. Friends. Such good friends you all are," Jinx said. "Stabbing each other in the back. Like Maddie did just today."

"I'm going. Perfect or not, I will not let my friends keep getting hurt."

Jackson saw it then—a shift in Jinx. He knew she respected that sort of thinking. Haley noticed too, and a look of pride came over her face.

Jinx lowered her arms and went back to packing the camera. "Grab that duffel bag and pack it in the car. We'll meet you out there. You need to do exactly as I say, got it?"

Haley nodded and grabbed the bag. She walked upstairs with it.

Jackson looked at Jinx, and Jinx said, "What?"

Jackson chuckled. "Nothing," he said. He just sort of appreciated his best friend more than anything in the world at that moment.

CHAPTER 12

It had been more than an hour, and the only thing the three had felt on the bridge was a damp sort of cold. Jinx shivered in her coat again, trying to avoid looking at Jackson and Haley while they held hands.

For the fifteenth time that night, she did an equipment check.

Nothing.

It was already 1:00 a.m., and Jinx started to think about calling it a night. She yawned, closed her eyes, and laid her head against a pillar, listening to the murmurs of Jackson and Haley. She could vaguely make out what they were saying as they leaned over the railing.

". . . it's what we should do, you know?"

"Yeah. I don't think it will get any better, do you?"

"The water is so peaceful . . ."

". . . just climb over . . ."

Jinx's eyes snapped open. A cloud had settled around Jackson and Haley as they huddled together. Tears streamed down Haley's face, and Jackson's shoulders were slumped again. It was happening.

Jinx looked at the EMF monitor in her hand—the needle spiked all the way to the red. The hair on the back of her neck stood up.

"Hey!" she yelled at Haley and Jackson, though they were right in front of her. "Hey! Snap out of it!"

Their expressions were dull and lifeless.

"You shouldn't have saved me, Jinx," Jackson said. "But now we can go ahead and do it." He looked at Haley and smiled grimly. "Come on."

Jinx shook her head in impatience, stepped up to Jackson, and swung her hand. As she connected with his face, the fire came back into his eyes. "That stung, Jinx!" he sputtered.

Jinx lifted her hand to slap Haley, too, but Haley grabbed her wrist. "Don't even think about it."

The cloud began moving slowly away from them. "There!" Jinx pointed. "We need to do something about this. Now."

Haley nodded. "Most definitely. No way is some stupid cloud going to make me feel this way again. Or any of my friends."

Jinx called out to the cloud, "Hey, you jerk! Why don't you pick on someone your own size!"

The cloud stopped moving. Jinx watched in amazement as the mist seemed to draw together—forming into a human-sized teen boy. He was gray and slightly transparent. This was the real deal. This was a real ghost. She looked at Haley and Jackson and saw their mouths were open too.

Jinx swallowed. She couldn't give up now. "Uh, yeah, stop bullying people!"

The figure walked toward them and laughed. The laugh seemed to echo all around them. "Me?" it said as it got closer. The boy was dressed in old-fashioned clothes from what looked like the fifties. He had on a shiny windbreaker coat, and his pants were high around his waist. His head seemed to lean to one side. "Me, bully? That's a laugh! *I'm* the one who was bullied! *I'm* the one who got picked on."

The ghost stepped within touching distance of Jinx. He had some major acne, and his hair stuck up all over the place. He wore big, thick glasses and talked with a nasal voice. But behind the glasses, the fury in his eyes made Jinx shake.

"I b-b-bet that was hard," she stammered. "Being bullied."

The ghost threw his hands up. "Yeah it was hard! So hard it killed me! Kids chased me to this bridge. Told me I was worthless. Told me I should jump."

Jinx gasped.

The ghost continued. "Every day from

seventh grade on, they'd beat me up, take my lunch money. All because I was different. I was a nerd. I got good grades and had bad skin and bad hair and didn't have the right clothes. Just because I wasn't some stupid follower, they picked on me every day!"

The ghost pushed his glasses up his nose. "All because of that, they chased me here. They made me climb over the railing and kept holding me over the water like they were going to let go."

Jinx dreaded what was coming.

"And then they did let go. My windbreaker slipped out of the stupid jock's hand. He never had trouble with a football, but I guess he couldn't hold on to me!"

He turned and looked at Jackson and Haley. "People like you did this to me." And then Jinx understood. He only targeted the popular people. Somehow he knew who they were. That's why the fog hadn't affected her. As they spoke, the fog began to rise once again, encircling Haley and Jackson. Jinx stepped closer to the ghost.

"No! You can't have them! I know you were hurt . . . And I'm so sorry for what those jerks did to you. But these two didn't do anything to you. Let them go."

Haley and Jackson swayed and stared off into the distance. Jinx wondered if they understood at all what was going on.

The ghost laughed. "They're all the same—they'll hurt someone too, mark my words. They'll do it to you! You're not like them. You'll be next."

"Look, I'm not winning any popularity contests, and I wouldn't hang with that crowd if I could," Jinx said. "People—any type of people—can be stupid around each other, especially in groups. But these two are different. Really. They're . . . good."

The ghost pointed at Haley. "Even her?"

Jinx thought for a minute and said, "Yeah. Even her." And she meant it. Haley had come to the bridge despite the danger to herself. She had wanted to help. And if Jackson liked her . . . well, that meant there was something to like. If they got out of this mess, maybe

Jinx would even apologize to Jackson for being so stubborn.

Doubtful, but she'd decide for sure later.

The ghost looked enraged. "*Fool!*" he yelled. "They'll only hurt you! You'll never be a part of their world!" And then he dissipated like a strong wind had blown him apart. The fog was gone.

Haley and Jackson blinked. "What happened?" Jackson asked.

Haley was shaking. "Is that ghost thing still here? I can't believe I almost jumped! Again!" Jackson put his arm around her.

Jinx felt alone. And very tired.

She remembered her camera and rewound the night's footage. It had captured nothing.

Sighing, she said, "Jackson, I think now would be a good time to do the cleansing ritual. Let's get rid of this thing once and for all."

Jackson nodded and grabbed his backpack. He took out a stick of sage and lit it. Then he began walking the bridge, murmuring words he'd learned on the Internet, leaving Haley and Jinx alone.

Haley looked at Jinx. "Thank you," she said. "I think you just saved my life."

Jinx shrugged. "All in a day's work."

As they left the bridge, Jinx thought she saw a gray fog hovering over the water. She wondered if they had truly gotten rid of the ghost.

CHAPTER 13

Jinx tapped one last command on her
computer.

There. Now Brian shouldn't be able to get
into the website. She couldn't believe she'd let
him in. She even erased his blog post—when
she read it over, she realized how truly creepy
it was.

Someone who wanted that much power
had some issues. In fact, he reminded her of
the ghost on the St. Johns Bridge. It sucked to
be picked on, for sure. But becoming a bully

yourself didn't make it right. She sighed.

Her e-mail dinged. It was from the Paranormalists site mailbox. Jinx's heart raced. Maybe it was a potential client! As scary as the ghost on the bridge had been, he was also exciting. Never before had Jinx seen such a phenomenon. And the camera didn't even pick him up! She would have to do some major research to figure out why not. In the meantime, she'd have to think of a better way to get documentation. She needed video for the website.

Jinx clicked to open up the e-mail:

Jinx,

It's Brian. I'm writing to you here because I know you've blocked me from your personal e-mail. And from your phone. Which I think is totally a lousy move, but I've come to expect it at this point.

I thought we had something, Jinx. I thought you were different. But you're just the same model of dumb robot as all the popular kids at school—you'll jump through

*any hoops to get their approval. I should
have known from the start since you were
friends with Jackson.*

   *After 5 new schools in 4 years, I guess
I'm the stupid one. Everyone is a conformo.
Including you.*

   *I won't bother you anymore since you've
made it so clear that you want to hang out
with your new (and old) popular friends.
That I'm not good enough.*

   *But I do want to tell you this: You'll
regret letting me go. I promise you. I'll
make you regret it.*

   Sleep tight,
   Brian

Jinx shivered as she reread the e-mail. She
would take ghosts over real, living people any
day. Especially psycho living people. She got
up and paced her room, touching her Pixies
poster for luck.

She sat down again and pressed forward.
She should let Jackson know about Brian's
message.

Then she stopped. She remembered how he'd looked when Brian came to her house. And she didn't want to put Jackson in danger if Brian was truly psycho. Most importantly, she could take care of herself.

Finally she hit the delete button.

Time for a new chapter for the Paranormalists, Jinx thought. No more Brians, no more angry bridge ghosts, no more grudges. Haley and she, if not exactly friends, had some mutual respect. Jackson and she were best friends again. Really, the world was as it should be.

Her e-mail dinged again. She opened the new message, half-expecting it to be from Brian.

Dear Paranormalists:

I think I know of a haunting and we need your help. Well, maybe not a haunting. Have you ever gotten rid of a spirit that's possessing someone?

I'm pretty sure that an evil spirit took hold of my little sister. I'm afraid she's going to hurt someone. Can you help us

before it's too late?
   Signed,
   Possessed in Portland

Jinx grinned to herself. Another case. Yep, all was right with the world.

What could possibly go wrong?

SEEK THE TRUTH
AND FIND THE CAUSE

WITH

THE PARANORMALISTS

CASE 1:
THE HAUNTING OF APARTMENT 101

Jinx was a social reject who became a punked-out paranormal investigator. Jackson is a jock by day and Jinx's ghost-hunting partner by night. When a popular girl named Emily asks the duo to explore a haunting in her dad's apartment, Jinx is skeptical—but Jackson insists they take the case. And the truth they find is even stranger than Emily's story.

CASE 2:
THE TERROR OF BLACK EAGLE TAVERN

Jinx's ghost-hunting partner Jackson may be a jock, but Jinx is not interested in helping his football buddy Todd—until Todd's case gets too weird to ignore. A supernatural presence is causing chaos at the bar Todd's family owns. And the threat has a connection to Todd that's deeper than even he realizes . . .

CASE 3:
THE MAYHEM ON MOHAWK AVENUE

Jinx and Jackson have become the go-to ghost hunters at their high school. When a new kid in town tries to get in on their business, Jinx is furious. Portland only needs one team to track down ghosties! But Jinx's quest to shut down her competition will lead her and Jackson down a dangerous path . . .

CASE 4:
THE BRIDGE OF DEATH

Jinx is the top paranormal investigator at her high school, and she has a blog to prove it. Jackson's her ghost-hunting partner by night—former partner, anyway. After a shakeup in the Paranormalists' operation, the two ex-best friends are on the outs, and at the worst possible time. Because a deadly supernatural threat is putting their classmates in harm's way . . .

AFTER THE DUST SETTLED

The world is over.
Can you survive what's next?